# About the author

Hovhannes Gevorgyan was born in 1987 in Armenia. He has a university degree in geography, political sciences and a doctoral dissertation in the field of history.

Gevorgyan is inspired by Christian theology, that's why he spent seven years in a monastery, living with monks.

He is passionate about travel, literature and architecture.

Gevorgyan is in favour of protecting the environment.

# THE PAINTER

# HOVHANNES GEVORGYAN

Translated from Armenian by Lusine Bostanjyan

---

## THE PAINTER

Vanguard Press

VANGUARD PAPERBACK

© Copyright 2022
**Hovhannes Gevorgyan**

The right of Hovhannes Gevorgayan to be identified as author of this work has been asserted by him in accordance with the Copyright, Designs and Patents Act 1988.

**All Rights Reserved**

No reproduction, copy or transmission of this publication may be made without written permission.
No paragraph of this publication may be reproduced, copied or transmitted save with the written permission of the publisher, or in accordance with the provisions of the Copyright Act 1956 (as amended).

Any person who commits any unauthorised act in relation to this publication may be liable to criminal prosecution and civil claims for damages.

A CIP catalogue record for this title is available from the British Library.

ISBN 978 1 80016 261 7

*Vanguard Press is an imprint of
Pegasus Elliot MacKenzie Publishers Ltd.*
www.pegasuspublishers.com

First Published in 2022

**Vanguard Press
Sheraton House Castle Park
Cambridge England**

Printed & Bound in Great Britain

# Foreword

The village was hidden in the forest hills. Only a few roofs and the dome of the ancient church, like islands, rose up from the green of the leaves. Every morning a drowsy priest silently pulled the ropes in prayer, and the forest gorge was filled with ringing of bells. The village was already awake. People were rushing about like ants, and they did not see the daily miracle. No one knew that in the sky at that very moment, awakened by the sound of the bells and sitting on the clouds, angels were watching the commotion in the small village. There in heaven, they were singing along with the priest's prayers in tune with the bells and counting the people rushing to the church.

The people were quickly crossing themselves, rushing out and walking through the muddy streets to their homes, sheds and schools, some — to the field or forest. White smoke from the stoves filled the village, covering it like fog. Viewed from afar, it could not even be noticed that there were people in the forest gorge. The dwellers of the gorge were born and lived dreaming of big cities — their lights, rich shops, where the streets were clean, and the work was not so hard and boring.

'There, in the city,' they said, 'people can walk along clean, beautiful streets, dine in fancy restaurants and be free. Nobody disturbs anyone and nobody knows anyone…'

# The Secrets of the Forest Hut

Meanwhile, far away from the gorge, Alexander was dashing along the road that stretched through the endless forests of distant Canada. Every now and then he looked at the monotonous blue forest and the dark sky, the beauty of which was being reflected in his glasses. His iron horse roared along the serpentine, drowning out the forest melody along with the music in the car. He had never been to the remote village or even heard of it before.

Alexander was born and brought up in a noisy city. At first glance, his penetrating gaze was striking. His dark brown eyes always looked straight ahead at people under his long eyebrows. He was tall, with a fair complexion and slightly curly black hair. Although Alexander was successful in his career and loved his hometown, the mountains pulled him out of Vancouver at every opportunity. Alone or with some of his few friends, Alexander liked hiking in the mountains. There was nothing more relaxing and exciting than being alone in nature under the starry sky. Only then could he be free and dream. Only by his tent, put up in the mountains, Alexander could sit for hours in front of the fire, watching the dancing flames. The air in the mountains was fresh and light; from there opened new horizons where he had never been and would never be. And the night…

The night there was different. It did not enfold, but rather fell with all its weight on his tent. It was enough to look up to return to childhood. The stars were shining brightly in the sky, enchanting, captivating the mind, forcing it to stop thinking. Alexander would lie for hours watching until his hand reached out to the open palm of the night, and sleep would close his eyes and unveil the visions of his dreams. He often saw his tent cut off from the Earth, floating with other planets along the heavenly path. He would open the tent door and see sparks of hot coal rising from the burning fire into the sky. They moved away like burning stars and disappeared somewhere. Without fail, he devoted all his days off to the mountains.

And that day, as always, he took the tent and everything he needed, put all the stuff in the car and decided to set off. He never decided the route in advance, and this time was no exception. Alexander preferred to leave the choice to chance. He just drove along unknown roads. He turned the wheel either to the right or to the left, sometimes spending the whole day on the road. In this way he was waiting for the moment when an attractive and mysterious island would appear. It always appeared in the form of a mountain or a hill and lured Alexander just with a sign familiar only to them.

The day was overcast, and the road ahead was getting wet with the first raindrops. It wound along the serpentine parallel to the river. Alexander was already quite far from his town. Cars were becoming less frequent. Everything seemed to be going well, until, as is often the case at the most inconvenient moment, on one of the bends the treacherous phone rang, and Alexander turned his attention to it. It took Alexander an instant to lose control. He realised immediately that this could be the end. Suddenly all sounds died away. He heard neither the phone nor the loud music. There was only the muffled heartbeat echo in his brain.

Before his eyes, the whole field of view quickly narrowed down to a single point and...

Alexander passed out. His car rolled into a gully, uprooting many trees until it crashed into an old oak tree. If the oak had not kept Alexander's car, it would have sunk into the river that flowed just below ...

'Teacher, I will plant my last tree here.'

There was inner conviction in Yaha's voice. He often surprised everyone with unexpected decisions. And even now, at that age, Yaha did not stop thinking and acting in a way that many did not understand, unlike his teacher, who knew him well and had taught him a lot. A sly gleam appeared in Yaha's eyes, as if he had something planned in his mind. People of his age usually don't have such shiny eyes. Elderly people tended to have a sad and tired look. But not Yaha. He had sparkling black eyes like an eagle. His broad shoulders could be seen underneath his traditional clothing, speaking of his great strength as a youth. In fact, he used to be the most successful hunter and the strongest man in his tribe. The old scars on his weak arms said a lot about his courage. There was a time when he could fight alone with a lynx, a wolf, even a bear.

'Why here, Yaha? It will be hard for the tree to hang over the river.'

'The river will take its fruit down to the valley. Much of it will get to the river bank and grow there.'

The teacher smiled with a kind smile as always. 'Then you need good fruit. Only strong seeds will grow on the rock.'

Saying this, he passed the acorn he had in his palm to old Yaha, who took it with his trembling hands and carefully covered it with poor soil.

'You will see, it will be very useful here. It will grow at all costs. Oak trees are strong, and the valley will be filled with them. One day you will see that this is the right place for it.'

Old Yaha was walking in these hills with his teacher for the last time. Sitting on a rock, they were discussing something important. When they finished, Yaha gave his little friend back to the teacher.

'Let Momo stay with you. I know, it's rude to return gifts, but Momo is no longer a gift. He is my inseparable friend, and I want to leave him with you.'

The teacher hugged Momo. He would remind him of his friendship with Yaha. Then they wished each other good luck, and the teacher promised not to turn back. Like all Native Americans, Old Yaha could feel the earth. He knew that his time was running out, and he decided to stay there, in the place where he had planted his last tree. The teacher kept his promise; he did not return to that slope for a long time. In the distance he could only see a giant oak tree, which, years later, every autumn, filled the river with hundreds of acorns. They were carried to the distant plains and, as Yaha had said, gave life to the valleys.

Many years had passed since then, and for some reason the teacher had been having the same dream for several days. He saw Yaha sitting under his oak tree. He wasn't sitting as usual; he seemed to be holding a giant tree with his shoulders and smiling silently. The teacher had been trying to unravel the dream but had no clue until the day when he found Momo sitting on Alexander's wrecked car after having looked for him everywhere. Momo, like all cats, was often missing, but always returned before dark. However, he had gone missing for the last two days, and that was yet another sign. Yaha's teacher immediately went to the rock hanging over the river. He silently looked at the crashed car, then at Momo, who was guarding it, and saw through all the signs. A familiar young man, whom he had already met in the mountains several months before, was trapped in the crashed car.

The sunbeams falling on Alexander's face from the window of the hut brought him to his senses. The headache was unbearable, his whole body was sore, and his legs were almost numb. Alexander tried to close his eyes, turn to the other side and see a new dream. In that noisy city, his sleep was often disturbed, so he would wake up with a headache and walk the streets for hours, or he would lie in bed until he fell asleep again. He soon realised that he was awake, and that what had happened was not a dream. *That was real*, he thought and began looking around. The unexpectedness of what he saw made him forget, for a moment, about the headache.

It was a small room, about seven feet long and five feet wide. He had never seen such pictures either in the sumptuously decorated temples of Rome, or in the palaces of Paris and Vienna. Even the greatest artists of the world would dream of having these colours in their paintings. In the centre of the ceiling there was a shining sun in the clouds, which spread bright colours across the ceiling and then smoothly down the walls. The walls themselves were covered in various beautiful landscapes, which were filled with and highlighted by the glow falling from the sun. On one side there were desert sands, which were gradually merging with the high alpine mountains. On the other side, rays falling from the ceiling penetrated deep into the forest, illuminating the trunks of the trees and the flowers scattered under them. The floor was dark blue, almost black, like a starry sky. A full moon was depicted in the centre, surrounded by stars and different planets, of which Alexander recognized only Saturn, or rather, its famous ring.

The light from the fireplace (in front of which he was lying) was dancing all over the room, and it seemed to Alexander that the images were alive and moving. He was looking around deliriously.

Directly in front of him there were an oval door and a small window looking like a long narrow arch. In the centre of the room there were two wooden chairs and a table. The table looked like a tree. Instead of legs, there was a beautiful tree trunk, the branches of which held a round table top. The chair looked like a small copy of the table. There was a jug on the table with a stick resembling a thin brush, and several thick books with some illegible writing. Alexander had never seen such letters. He was lying in front of the hot fire, which resembled a Russian stove, but with the exception that there was a large opening in the front, like in a fireplace.

The fireplace was red-hot; Alexander felt pleasant warmth all over his body. The white stones near the opening had got pinkish from the heat, but the thin rope blanket on which Alexander was lying left most of the heat, on the stones, underneath.

Alexander had not noticed a small chest of drawers by his feet, which stood parallel to the fireplace. It was wooden, decorated with ornaments of various fruits and animals. It had three horizontal drawers with ball-shaped handles.

After a while, the headache came back again, and the man thought that he probably had a concussion. While he was thinking about who had brought him there and how, and whose house it was, he felt something moving under the fireplace. For some reason he was frightened. For the first time, Alexander found himself helpless and weak. He held his breath for a moment, he could not even blink in fear, but instantly came to senses, trying to judge soberly. *Whoever it is... If he wanted to hurt me, I would not be lying here now.* He turned to the floor and coughed softly.

A giant white cat slowly and indifferently appeared from under the fireplace and headed for the table. The cat did not even look at the fireplace, walked up to the table, lightly jumped on it, stretched itself, and then turned over and lay with its back to Alexander. It was a house cat, completely white apart from the tail. But there was something strange about it. The cat was about twice the size of a normal cat and looked rather weird in that room.

'Kitty, kitty,' Alexander called the cat anxiously.

The cat bent its head to the side, looked at Alexander with dark green eyes, very cold and indifferent. Then it slowly got up, jumped off to the floor, stood on its hind legs and walked up to the door. It pulled the handle decisively, opened the door slightly, left a paw on the handle, put the other on its hip and leaned against the door. Just like a human. Alexander was confused.

The cat could walk on its hind legs, open doors, and behaved as if it were a human.

'Hey, are you listening to me?' Alexander shouted. 'I'm talking to you, look at me!'

But the cat just wagged its tail to the left and to the right with complete indifference. Alexander tried to stand up. His legs were too weak, and he realised that it was beyond his power. A little later, he noticed some movement in the forest. His eyes were wide open. 'Hmm, who is this?' Alexander thought, when he saw someone approaching the hut from the trees. From afar, he could only see a moving figure in the forest dim. Soon the figure came up to the door. The cat happily approached him on all fours, and they entered together. The stranger closed the door, stroked the cat, and went to the fireplace.

'Lie down, lie down! I see you are recovering,' he said to Alexander in a calm but hoarse voice. He was a tall man with a slightly dark face. He wore dark blue clothes that looked like a priest's robe. The robe looked quite good on the stranger, falling from shoulders to ankles. He had nothing on his feet, no shoes, nothing at all. At the waist, two parallel thin gold ropes served as a strong belt. The stranger might be in his fifties, with hair and a short beard full of grey hair. The bushy eyebrows were almost completely white. Beneath them, his deep blue eyes radiated extraordinary warmth.

Neither the stranger's clothes nor his neat face and hair indicated that he was a forest dweller. He walked with a knightly gait, but at the same time, very careful and light, like his giant cat. Only lions have this combination of strength and elegance in nature. As he approached and put his warm hand on Alexander's head, the man felt strange warmth. All fears and doubts vanished. Alexander kept trying to catch the man's gaze and to look deeper into his eyes, but the stranger's eyes were evasive as if on purpose. He bent down in front of the fireplace, and Alexander heard the sound of water. As he was about to ask a question, the stranger held out a heavy clay mug decorated with beautiful flowers.

'This is a potion. It will help you get well soon and relieve your headache.'

Having said this, he immediately turned around, took a book from the top drawer of the chest, like the ones he had on the table, and went up to it.

Meanwhile, Alexander finally gathered his thoughts and said, 'Thank you very much, sir. My name is Alexander. I…'

He was about to finish when the cat pulled out a yellowish candle-like cylinder from the top drawer. He calmly walked to the fireplace on his hind legs, lit it, then just as calmly took it to his master and handed it to him. The stranger took the candle, put it in front of himself and stroked the cat.

Seeing this, Alexander got frightened. He even felt a tremor in his hands. *Is he a wizard? How come a cat be not afraid of fire, and what is more...* he thought, then blurted out, 'Who are you? What does all this mean? What do you want from me? Where am I?'

Alexander could continue asking questions for a long time, realizing deep in his heart, that this was not what he wanted to ask.

Meanwhile, without taking his eyes off the book, the host took down some notes with a stick from the jar resembling a brush and said very calmly, 'I am who I am. And this means that you are alive, and you are in my hut. I want you to get well soon. But what Momo wants from you, alas, I don't know. Well, you can ask him.' Sitting at the master's feet at that moment, the cat mewed, and the stranger, smiling slightly under his breath, added, 'Ah, yes, and Momo told me when I came in, that he didn't want you to call him 'kitty'.'

The stranger spoke as if he were answering a simple question of a man-child. He did not even take his eyes off the book, sparingly uttering a few words to the frightened and surprised guest.

Alexander got even more frightened. 'What does it mean — I am who I am? How can Momo light a candle and talk to you?' he asked emphatically. 'Are you a wizard? Who has sent you?'

Alexander was not worried about the stranger or his cat, but about his condition. He was very weak and almost motionless. The sense of helplessness and weakness gripped him from within. Despite the infinite kindness that reigned in that room, there was still something strange about it, and the behaviour of the stranger increased the suspicions of the young man. The host continued ignoring his questions, and this offended his pride. Soon, Alexander stopped asking questions. The stranger kept on writing, turning the pages back and forth. His cat was looking at Alexander calmly but enquiringly and just as calmly wagging its tail. The monotony of the room was relieved when the mysterious host finished writing.

'Hmm, yes,' he mumbled under his breath, and after the last stroke he put the brush into the jug. Then he took up the book, blew on the page to dry the ink, and finally closed it. He stood up and put the book down.

'A wizard? What is a wizard?' suddenly the host asked, naively and sincerely. For a moment, Alexander almost believed that the old man really didn't understand what he had meant, ss if he had heard a new word and was waiting for an explanation. But Alexander was very scared and really surprised by what he saw. He was waiting for an explanation himself. It was obvious that their conversation did not go well, as if they spoke different languages. At last, the host got up wearily, turned to the door and said, 'Since you are in my bed, I will spend the night in my other hut, and in the morning you should feel better. Momo will stay here, take care of you until dawn. And now, drink the potion. It is not very useful when it is cold.'

Having said this, he turned to the cat, gave it a look, then blew out the candle and left the hut. Alexander went on speaking, wagged his finger and tried to keep up the conversation. But all in vain. The stranger said no more. Nothing could be heard in the hut except for the fire and the muffled sounds of the forest. The young man was silent. Momo curled up on the chest of drawers and closed his eyes.

Alexander had never felt so insecure. *I am in a fairy hut built in the forest with this strange cat and a crazy old man, almost completely motionless and helpless. But for some reason, these two seem so close to me. What should I do?* he thought, realizing that there was nothing in his hands, but the mug of the tasty-smelling potion.

*Um, come what may*, he thought, and felt the incredible flavor of the drink in his mouth. It tasted very pleasant and fresh already in the throat. Alexander sensed something pure fill his body. In a strange way, he felt how the miracle cure was flowing with the blood in his veins. After a few sips, Alexander felt better, and he emptied the mug with the dark red drink insatiably, in one breath and realised that he was recovering. The headache had dulled, and he felt relieved.

The night in the forest was very peaceful. The wind was blowing over the green of the trees, and the first autumn leaves were falling. Soon under the sound of the flame, the young man's eyes closed, and he fell asleep.

It was already noon when Alexander woke up from a deep sleep. When he opened his eyes and saw the painted walls and the ceiling, he didn't believe for a second, that what had happened was true. He was alone. A good night's sleep had worked well for him. And the potion worked a real miracle. Alexander had recovered fully, moreover, he had never felt so energetic before. It seemed a real wonder. The day before he was still motionless and in unbearable pain. And now there was not even a trace of the accident left, not even the bruises. Alexander was taken aback but did not feel bitter towards the stranger any more. He hoped to sort things out as soon as possible. He was as jolly as a sandboy. Alexander had regained his strength and energy. He got up and hoped to see the cat under the fireplace, but in vain; there was no one in the room. Walking with infirm steps, he went up to the door.

The forest was very beautiful. In front of the hut there was a small meadow, bright and green, and the hut itself was overgrown with vines. Alexander walked around the house and found nothing that could interest him. In the far corner, under the roof, there was a large barrel, where rainwater apparently was collected. He leaned over it and found that the water was clean, suitable not only for washing, but also for drinking. Then he sat down on the doorstep, confident that the old man would soon appear. Alexander was no longer afraid. He was sure the old man would not harm him. Firstly, he had the feeling, and secondly, Alexander realised that he owed him his life and health. By no means had the young man's cautiousness vanished, but deep inside Alexander decided to make friends with that mysterious person in order to find out the secret of the potion. How could that remedy have healed such wounds just overnight? Besides, Alexander guessed who the author of the illustrated room was, but he would like to see and learn more.

When Alexander got tired of waiting, he decided to go inside and find a clue in the hut. When he entered, his first gaze fell on the books of the day before.

Under the dark brown wooden case were thick pages with some illegible writing. He had never seen such letters before. In the tables covering the pages, the inscriptions resembled a calculation.

In thick, flowing lines, the letters were drawn rather than written. They were not like any other alphabet. Some of the inscriptions were made in black, others in light or dark green ink. It was also impossible to find any hidden meaning in the starry sky on the floor. Everything was incomprehensible and mysterious. It even seemed to Alexander that the sun on the ceiling was brighter at that moment than the day before. And it looked as if the clouds weren't as many. But he quickly dismissed the idea, since even in that mysterious hut, it would seem incredible if the painted images could have changed overnight.

Alexander was walking around the room, looking at the ground and trying to find an explanation. He stopped on the idea pieced together in his human sensible mind, according to which a young man who had fainted after an accident was accidentally found and brought into the house by a man who was probably one of the adventurers fleeing civilization. Undoubtedly, he was a kind, intelligent and gifted person. Alexander had a vivid imagination and could imagine everything, but he had never believed in witches and wizards. All that was so strange for him. And the most amazing thing was the potion, which had cured him overnight, but there was an explanation for that as well.

Momo was also beyond human understanding, but circus animals could perform even harder tricks. Thus, Alexander decided that, apparently, Momo was a purebred and well-trained cat. So, he should stop worrying about it too much.

He was so absorbed and deep in his thoughts, that he didn't notice Momo, until he was already in the doorway. That made him happy. If the cat came, the owner should soon appear as well. Momo was as confident as ever. He walked across the hall very contentedly, holding his long tail high, as if he was marching in a military parade. A few steps from the fireplace, he jumped on his favourite spot and struck a pose. He looked at the young man with his dark green eyes, as if he was waiting to hear something important from him.

'I see you have already recovered.'

Alexander turned to a familiar voice and saw the stranger at the door. He was holding a pipe in one hand and a small cloth bag in the other.

'Your potion works wonders. Look, I've completely recovered, and couldn't feel better. Won't you reveal your secret? I want to know who you are, by all means. Please, tell me what I can do to repay…'

'No, no, don't go on! First, it was Momo who helped you, and help shouldn't be repaid. Never ever! Finally, you have nothing that could be of interest for Momo. The king of cats has the most noble attitude of all animals. Don't even try to persuade him.'

The host interrupted him decisively but calmly, so that the young man did not have time to introduce himself. Alexander looked in surprise at Momo, who was lying on the fireplace at that moment. There was not even a hint of nobility in giant Momo. He lay back with his white fat belly up, listening attentively to the conversation between the two men. And maybe that's why the last words of the master seemed quite ridiculous to Alexander.

Alexander had a feeling that the conversation would most likely fail again. But this time he showed respect and, most importantly, trust in the old man. Alexander was determined and willing to be patient. Besides, he was full of gratitude and kindness to return favour. That was why, he had to try his best to understand the mysterious stranger.

'Now, I'll make rosehip tea for you,' the host continued.

He took two large handfuls of rosehips from the bag, threw them into a pot of water and hung it over the fire.

Alexander thanked the old man once again for saving him, the medicine and the tea. Out of courtesy, he thanked Momo as well. He said that he lived in Vancouver and told him how he had crashed.

'And yours? What's your name?' the old man asked unexpectedly, as if he had already revealed his name.

'Alexander Constantine Pellegrini,' he answered happily, 'and what about yours?'

At that moment, a slight sadness was reflected on the old man's face.

With a puzzled look he shrugged his shoulders and seriously responded that he had no name. Different people in different times called him by different names. His friend, Yaha, had called him Teacher, and people in the Sahara called him Dervish and by many other names.

'How can a person not have a name?'

Alexander asked many questions which the old man intentionally seemed to ignore. He wondered what he could tell the young man and how. When they sat down to drink tea, the old man finally decided to give it a try. He knew that nothing happened by accident, and that Momo would not have approached everyone. In addition, he had seen Alexander once before. After all, his job was to help people, so he decided not to reject Alexander.

'A few days ago, I had a dream — the oak tree, into which your car crashed. It was recurring for several days. I saw one of my old friends holding the tree on his back. In the beginning, I didn't understand what it meant, but then Momo disappeared. He didn't show up for two days. At first, I thought that something had happened to him, but later I remembered my dream and immediately headed for that place. Momo was sitting on your car and was guarding you. I don't know why, but he decided to save you at all costs, and then my dream showed some interconnectedness as well. I got you out of the car and brought you here.'

The old man did not tell Alexander that his dreams always came down from heaven, and that Alexander himself was chosen by heaven. He didn't say it because, firstly, Alexander wouldn't understand, and secondly, he wouldn't believe it. The old man knew people well, and first he had to understand why Alexander had been chosen. He hadn't had such signs for many years and had never been so close to anyone. So far, there had been no one in his hut to drink tea with him. The old man realised that saving the young man was not the only mission. But he didn't know what exactly he could do, and that made the task more difficult.

You had to be very careful with people. They were like children, weak and fragile, but at the same time, unlike children, adults were confident in themselves. Alexander, like everyone else, was curious — he wanted to know for the sake of knowing. And the old man knew that one could not say all as it was. He knew that people wanted to open and enter all the closed doors and hearts with great carelessness. And when curious things drew their attention, they instantly left and forgot everything that they wanted to discover. And it caused him a lot of suffering, but that was the reality.

At the same time, the old man knew that the world rested on the shoulders of good and virtuous people, and that without them it was impossible to achieve great things. In ancient times, the world was even depicted on the backs of elephants and turtles. It was symbolic that the ancient people knew more, that's why they used elephants and turtles as symbols of human virtue. Later many people forgot about it and even laughed at it, considering the ideas of their forefathers ridiculous. And Atlas? After all, he was also the symbol of great human power who carried the weight of the entire universe on his shoulders.

The old man knew that. He knew a lot about people, and now one of them was sitting in front of him, waiting for his words. *I have a big responsibility*, the old man thought, looking at Alexander's eyes burning with curiosity. The sparkle in those eyes depended on him. Would they shine with love and joy, would he know more than he did, or…?

The old man knew that it would be impossible to deceive him, as adults usually deceived children. It was out of the question, and made things harder, but he knew that the young man would not ask what he was not ready to know. He would ask what people usually asked, and everything would end easily. But the problem was not in the end, but in the beginning.

'You'd better tell me about yourself,' said the old man, suddenly, with a very cheerful smile. 'As you can see, I rarely have guests. What's your life like?'

Alexander did not know what to start with and decided to tell about himself in a few words. He talked about his family, where they were from and what they did. Then he spoke in detail about his work. He worked for a large and powerful company. Although he tried not to show it, either his voice or his eyes betrayed his pride. The old man quickly felt an instant change in Alexander's face, as he spoke of his position. Then the old man learnt that Alexander loved hiking in the mountains and staying there alone for a while. That, the old man had already guessed. Alexander did not speak long. He told the truth, but the old man did not seem to be impressed. According to him, Alexander was a lonely and ordinary man who carefully concealed the most important of all his virtues, so that people would not think that he was weak. People have always been like that, but talking to Alexander, the old man realised that they had become more reserved. They were afraid that their kindness and straightforwardness would harm them, and for that very reason they kept them away from strangers, opening their hearts only to the closest ones.

Alexander was telling ordinary things, but the old man seemed to be listening to the story of all mankind. He didn't want to show it, but what he heard aroused deep disappointment in the old man's heart. His world was different, as were his priorities. He lived without the boundaries that people set for themselves. He was beyond the human system. He lived in a completely different environment of insiders and outsiders. But the old man knew that not all of them were dormant and reserved. In addition, he knew that there was a lot of pressure on the people, and it was not always them who created difficulties for themselves.

He understood that it was hard to walk the path alone, but it was much harder to do it together if not everyone started from the beginning. After all, people follow in the footsteps of their ancestors, but not only have they not seen, but also not heard of their first steps. If they only knew where they came from and where they were going, they would probably be more assertive. But man was like a butterfly; he started a new life every day, with the only difference that the human day is much longer than the day of the butterfly. The old man witnessed the first steps and decisions of the people, but the day was not over for him. He had been watching them like a witness forever. Meanwhile, they lost the reasons for their first decisions and got lost.

Squirrels know that they need to stock up for the winter, and they do, but memory plays a bad trick on them. They forget about the place they stock most of their winter supplies, and it turns out that they have been working hard for several days in vain. Today people are like those squirrels who, having lost some of their greatest gifts, instinctively continue to hurry somewhere and build something. The stranger, of course, would like people to be like wise elephants and long-living turtles. But that is not the case.

'Well, how do *you* live? Why are you alone? Why in the forest?' asked Alexander, having finished talking about himself. Hearing the questions, the old man looked surprised. It seemed as if Alexander had asked him about something forbidden, and it both surprised and slightly offended him.

'Alone? How can you be alone in the forest? It is impossible to be alone in the forest.'

'Well, I mean wild nature and wild animals. How long have you been living like this?'

The old man had an expression of irritation on his face. He immediately interrupted Alexander, saying that nature could not be wild. People had become wild. How could he call something wild of which he was a part? Didn't man destroy wildlife and satisfy all his needs at the expense of nature? And animals had not been wild at all, they became wild because of the man.

'If there is something wild in the world, then it is not a creature. Neither the man nor animals. A savage has wild manners, and this is how a human can live.'

'I could hardly live in the forest. The city gives me work, my home is there... But you didn't tell me anything, about yourself, why?' Alexander broke the awkward silence.

'What do you want to know?'

'I want to know who you are, where you come from and how you were able to cure me so quickly. How is it that animals do not harm you?'

'Okay, but why do you need it?'

'I want to know the truth.'

'What is the truth for you?'

'I think it is something like light, and there is more light, in your world.'

'If you love light, then you will find the truth by yourself. But you must love it with all your heart so that nothing gets in its way. You think there is more light in my world, but you prefer your world. It gives you a job; your home is there, isn't it? If so, then you do not love light with all your heart.'

Alexander was upset for a moment. He didn't know what to say. The old man's words were true, but he wanted to know more.

'It's because I don't know much about your world. But I would like to learn from you, if you would teach me.'

'I can help you discover the world, but you must find the truth in it on your own. Only you can find it, and it will stay with you forever.'

Alexander was sure of one thing, that this time it was serendipity that he had crashed his car. He considered meeting such a person an exceptional opportunity and wanted to learn more and stay longer with him. Who would have thought that this could happen? He had been asking for a long time until the old man, tired of Alexander's voice, finally spoke up. He decided to start from the beginning, but on the strict condition that the young man would not interrupt him and would listen to the end.

'If only you could listen,' the old man said mysteriously and continued, 'People are withdrawn, so they cannot hear, and they can learn to speak after they hear. But try to hear me and to listen to me. I know a lot about you. I know that you love freedom, but like many, you have no choice. Your soul loves it, but you are closed, like all people. You are looking for what you lost long ago, and if you want, I will help you find it. But first, you must promise to follow my terms. First, never tell anyone about me and what I'm going to teach you. Secondly, do not be afraid of yourself when the time comes.'

Alexander did not quite understand what the second condition was about, but he agreed out of curiosity and the old man went on,

'He created people in his own image and gave Adam many virtues. People oversaw the entire Garden of Eden, knew how to read nature, and animals trusted them. But when people started to leave and withdraw, everything changed. The sons of Adam gradually forgot their virtues and reserved themselves. They stopped protecting the nature and began to destroy it. Further and further they went, fleeing the shelters they had built. Then He created us to help the man and to preserve the forests. Otherwise, people would destroy themselves. It was the eighth day. I got the north, and my brother got the south.'

For a moment Alexander took the stranger for a madman, but decided not to interrupt him, and the stranger continued rather seriously.

'When Gilgamesh cut down the last gardens of Eden and built Uruk, I went further north and filled endless fields with forests. Then people began building larger cities and separating themselves from the world with large stone walls. So, they started to fight with what they were called upon to protect. Adam was given the ability to give names, but since we were created later, when his sons had already lost that gift, we did not receive a name. Different people have given us different names.'

Alexander listened with great interest to everything the old man said. He was talking very vividly, describing everything in detail. Before his eyes rose giant Gilgamesh, who was second to none in the world.

No one could compete with him in strength or courage. He saw Uruk being built and separated from the world by walls. The expanding city glorified its master, and Gilgamesh became more and more reserved from the rest. In the end, after realizing his mistake and seeing the golden bull, he had a battle with himself. But the hero who had defeated everyone could not win over himself. He could not destroy what was being built on his orders. He could not demolish the temple of his glory and scatter it all over the world. The golden bull was in that temple, and all his fears and weaknesses were chained there.

So, countless stonecutters hit the stones with their hammers, polished them and stacked them on top of each other to build the temple. The days were going by, and the walls were thickening. Meantime, the golden bull kept on growing and conquering the hearts of people. And then the moment came when the bull completely possessed them. Gilgamesh saw this and eventually decided to fight. The fear was great, but the hero raised his hands to the sky, and his heart was filled with heaven. He got stronger and more clear-minded. Gilgamesh jumped on the bull and the battle started...

The king of Uruk was trying to overthrow the bull for a long time. He firmly held the bull's golden horns in his mighty hands, but it was steady as a rock. For the first time, Gilgamesh lost and fell to his knees. The desperate giant looked up at the sky again, and the sky listened to him for the second time. Enkidu from the north cheered him up. People quickly forgot about the bull. But Enkidu realised that fear had already taken root in the hearts of the people, and that they could drive it away only by themselves.

And no matter how much he fought the bulls and defeated them, new bulls were born. In the end, people were left alone on the path of their fears and ordeals. But this path sharpened the existing contradictions, leading them to a conflict between the spiritual and earthly worlds. They wanted to reach heaven, because they thought the Earth was already theirs. They started building a tower, and the more bricks there were, the more the hearts of people closed. They became so proud and cut off from the world that they even began to withdraw from each other. And one day they began to misunderstand each other. Languages were mixed and divided people into different nations. But He saved them by destroying the tower, and people were scattered in different parts. Alexander saw Babylon in all its glory, as well as all the other cities and their people that were no longer part of the nature.

The old man said that he was fighting and helping people, but they were already too scattered and did not hear. Therefore, he too slowly isolated himself from people, fighting alone for the good of the world. Very rarely did people with open souls find him, and he talked to them. The old man said that he remembered every tree he had planted, and that he spoke to trees which he considered his children. He said that with every new forest cut down, he lost his strength and his hair turned grey. And when forests were gone, perhaps, he wouldn't exist any more. Alexander was listening with great interest, but the old man's words were hard to believe. The old man knew this, but he kept on telling incredible things about conversations with trees as he walked through the forest, that they told him everything: how long they had been waiting for the sunrise to be able to reach the sun and how difficult it was to fight the wind. He also spoke with animals, who he never called beast or savage.

'Today only mountains can endure. People haven't reached the mountains yet, and therefore, the last islands of freedom can be found in the mountains. That's why you like to escape there, but you do return to the city, where you keep your fears and grace locked away.'

Alexander listened without interrupting, even though every now and then there were questions he would like to ask, which in his view, the old man would not be able to answer. But whenever he wanted to do that, he remembered that he could not interfere, and he sipped his rosehip tea instead.

Then he learned that the books with strange inscriptions were registers in which the old man kept taking notes. The lost trees were registered in black ink and the newly planted ones in light green. The real forest was marked dark green. The old man could speak for a long time, and tell about things which Alexander would not believe. He knew that and could read it in his guest's eyes. This was not the first time when people did not believe the reality.

*Well, I've had enough of telling him what he does not believe. People are people. To make them believe you, they always need a miracle as a proof*, thought the old man and decided to give Alexander what inevitably was given to a man. But, firstly, he let the young man speak up and didn't have to wait long for the questions.

Alexander had already forgotten about the potion. The things he had just heard were more unbelievable, and he was close to the thought, that the old man was simply mad. The fact that the old man could have seen him in the mountains, meant nothing to Alexander. Anyone could have seen him there.

Alexander was convinced that the old man had made it all up, and that it did not make sense to talk to him about what he had just heard. Anyway, he decided to continue the conversation. 'So, according to you, man was created to be a gardener, wasn't he? Don't you agree that art and beauty are created in the city? Without them, there would be no development. Just imagine the world without the great art.'

The old man obviously did not like Alexander's ironic question, but he did not express his disagreement and said, 'In the beginning, God created the sky and the earth. The earth was empty and had no form, Alex. You cannot even imagine what the Earth looked like, let alone what it means that it was empty and shapeless. But you should know that people have played a great role in filling and decorating it. You have been given the earth not for your personal needs, but as a mission. Angels serve in heaven, and you must take care of the world. The Earth is not just a planet, this is the centre of the Universe, its heart. And in its centre, there is man. If you do not fulfil your mission and do not fill the world, you will be useless and very soon become extinct.

'And this is not just gardening,' he continued. 'There is the Earth, and there is heaven, and one of them was entrusted to you. But you are closed and do not care what that means. And I cannot explain it to you unless you have learnt to listen.'

Alexander really could not understand it. He saw the world like others, just like it was. He did not know which words were given names by Adam. He knew names but their essence was unknown to him. To perceive them he had to open himself up first, as the stranger had said.

'Do you mean that you were made by the Creator on the eighth day and have been living since Gilgamesh's times? What does it mean to be closed, and why do you think people are closed?'

The old man was looking for simple words in his mind to be able to explain the inexplicable. After a short pause, he continued calmly, 'Yes, that's true. People have closed themselves, because they are not free any more. Even now, when they want to deprive a man of his freedom, they imprison him, close him somewhere.

So, you are closed, because you have lost your freedom.'

'And what is freedom?'

'To be free is to be responsible. Only a responsible person can be free, and people have failed in this. They don't care that the world is sinking. And if man is required to answer for it, he will be destroyed as well. The soul knows about it; that's why it has closed itself from the body. You are always thinking about the end of the world, but you yourselves will cause it.'

Alexander listened attentively. Deep down he understood everything but could not believe it.

'It's like love. The more women you have in your life, the less you understand what love is. Don't you agree? If you really loved, you would love your one and only, and there wouldn't be the other. But, as long as there is the second one, the both of them are imperfect. The former excludes true love for the latter and vice versa. That's the case with your great art. You remember about it from time to time and then say goodbye to it. Art and beauty sparkle, but do not burn.'

Hearing about art, Alexander again turned his attention to the room. He decided to ask about the paintings, which were too beautiful for the eye to get used to them. Besides, he wanted to put the conversation at ease a little bit. It was likely to turn into a philosophical polemic, which the young man did not wish at all.

'How did you manage to paint all this? Where did you get such colours?'

The old man's deep blue eyes smiled tenderly but shrewdly at the young man. 'Well, as you can see, there is great art also in the forest, because it is born thanks to the soul, and not civilisation. Virtues are given from above like a miracle. They illuminate the darkness like a burning star, generously and relentlessly sending their light into infinity. Instead, darkness gives them nothing. Stars are burning, and even death cannot stop them. They sacrifice their last bit of light and die. But He who gave this light gives life to a new star, and it again explodes out of nothing and shines brighter than before. Virtue is like light, and a star is like the man.

'Well, I have some virtues, too. If you want, I can show you more. Just don't be afraid of yourself,' he added.

Alexander smiled and assured the man that he would not be scared. The old man had no intention of surprising or showing off. He just gave Alexander what could help him. Such he was, distant and bright like a star, and those who approached him by the will of his Lord received his light and warmth.

'Well, then look,' said the old man, standing in the centre of the room.

He raised his hands to the ceiling, took a deep breath, and blew with force. Small golden rays shone on the ceiling, and when the old man moved his hands, the clouds around the sun fully exposed it. The walls of the room were filled with its light, and the shades of the walls became lighter. Then the old man blew softly, and the clouds began to glide over the ceiling. A minute or two later, he raised his hands once more, this time piecing together the snow-white clouds so that the animated sky turned back into a painting again.

Alexander was not scared; he was happy. He was so fascinated that he could not help but smile wide and was lost for words. The old man also smiled. Guests were very rare at his place, and he surprised very few of them with his little miracles. He experienced the joy of the author, who felt appreciated. Everything was confused in Alexander's head, and he no longer knew what to think. His mind had simply given up.

'Please, forgive me, you are a real master. In the beginning, I did not believe your words, but now… I do not believe my eyes, and the walls, the walls come to life too.'

Alexander was as happy as a child. He wanted to stay with the stranger with all his heart, listen to him and learn from him. For Alexander, the old man was no longer crazy, and his words were not delirious any more. It was like a dream for him. Although there was no witchcraft, it was like magic. At that moment, he felt like in his childhood, where everything was possible.

The old man laughed and went up to Alexander. He stood with his back to the desert depicted on the wall. The old man stretched out his hands and touched it. When thin golden rays fell on the wall, he blew and slid his palms over it. It seemed that the wall would open itself up, revealing a passage to other worlds. But that did not happen. Instead, a light breeze blew from the desert directly towards Alexander. The colour of the sand and the sky changed. They were different from what they were before. The sky was orange, and the sand was dark. The old man took a step and walked into the sands.

'Come on, Alex! It is only dawn in the Sahara, don't be afraid. Come with me.'

It seemed to Alexander that nothing could surprise him, but the old man kept astonishing him, and he had a feeling that this was not the end. He took a cautious step and, just a foot away from the dense Canadian forest, found himself in Africa. When he was standing on the sand and saw the endless desert, he was frozen for a moment. Alexander was petrified even in his thoughts. But the light breeze whispered that it was not a dream. He bent down, picked up a handful of cold sand, turned back and saw the endless desert just awakening from a night's sleep.

'The hut, the hut has disappeared… Look…!'

He ran after the old man. When he reached him, he assured Alexander that the hut had not disappeared — it was the young man who did not see it.

'Come on, I'll show you my new garden, which I want to plant.'

'There is no water here, is there?'

'There *is* water… It's under the sand.'

Together they climbed a sand hill, from which there was a magnificent view. In the heart of the desert, on the rocky hills, there was a small oasis. Below, at the bottom of one of the slopes, a small stream found its source. It ran across the tiny green island and disappeared in the sand. It was a vital lifeline along which, just three or four feet away, grew palm trees and figs. Alexander realised that they were planted and taken care of by his new friend. The opposite side of the hill was also rocky, and it took half an hour to get to the palm trees.

Alexander learned what to do to expand the oasis. It was hard work. It was necessary to dig a deep ditch along the stream and to pile up stones and dig out poor soil on the bank of the stream. Only after filling the ditch up with all the dry leaves and branches, could you plant new trees and water them generously. Alexander understood that in this way the moisture would stay in the ditch longer, and the seedlings would not dry out even in the arid desert climate. And when they grew and reached with their roots the water buried under the sand, they would no longer need any care. In their shade, new ditches could be dug, filled with dry leaves, and so on.

Palm trees grew and filled a part of the desert with their greenery. The green island of the old magician surrounded by the sea of golden sands was incredibly beautiful. The wind carried dust waves from the Sahara to the oasis. But these waves crashed against the solid boundaries of the old man's green island. It was cool in the shade of the palm trees, and any survivor of a shipwreck in this sand sea could find life there.

Alexander didn't notice the sun rise from behind the hills and fill with its warmth the desert which had cooled overnight. Alexander was working obsessively with the old man, asking questions and listening to the things he had never heard of or even imagined. Then, when the sun was high, they finished their work and climbed the hill. Once again from that spot they threw their glance at the green island and headed for the desert.

It was the first time Alexander had seen such beauty. The splendour of the desert was beyond ordinary; there was something symbolic in it. And he seemed to guess why the old man had brought him there. It reminded him of what they were talking about in the hut. 'Beauty doesn't necessarily mean goodness and life. Beauty itself is nothing if it does not fill you up and radiate goodness.' Well, the desert was beautiful, but deadly at the same time. And Alexander realised that more and more people were creating such beauty. He began to understand the language of the old man.

'Doesn't the sand burn your feet?'

'I like feeling the warmth of the sun under my feet. It gives me strength,' the old man replied with a smile, and then motioned for him to stop.

He raised his hands and blew, and Alexander saw golden rays, and soon he was inside the hut again. When they were entering, Alexander found that it was already evening in the forest. He was tired and wanted to sleep, but he did not want to part with the old man. They lit the fire, the old man took notes in his books, and then wished him goodnight.

He left the hut and soon disappeared behind the trees. Alexander stayed with Momo. After all this, he looked at Momo differently. Alexander began telling him everything he had seen. Momo was listening to him sitting on the fireplace, and this time Alexander saw sympathy and trust in his eyes. They became friends that evening. Alexander couldn't sleep for a long time. He was afraid that if he closed his eyes, the dream would immediately vanish, and he would wake up somewhere else.

Although Alexander had not planted any trees until he met the old man, he enjoyed working the soil. He felt that he had left a piece of his heart there, in the warm sands, with the palm trees that he had planted. He wondered for a long time whether his trees would grow or dry up, whether people would sit under their shade… Alexander didn't know that. He knew he wanted to go there at least once again and hear the unnamed old man talking to the palm trees.

The white giant (that's what Alexander called Momo) was lying on his chest and purring like all cats. Although he was huge, and his presence made Alexander breathe heavily, Momo did not touch his new friend. After all, it was Alexander, lying in Momo's place; besides, he enjoyed the fact that the white giant trusted him.

It was early when he woke up and left the hut. Although there was no rain at night, the forest looked well washed. He felt the air of freshness on his face. There were no bushes under the trees, because the old man liked it when the forest was neat and tidy. Like an architect, he planned the place for every tree and shrub, as if foreseeing the forest in years ahead. He spoke to the forest in the language of nature. Alexander admired the forest, which looked like the Garden of Eden.

Shortly thereafter, the grey-haired old man in a blue robe appeared from behind giant brown trunks. He was walking slowly, without taking his eyes off the ground. White smoke was rising from his pipe, merging with the same white of his beard. Only when he had reached Alexander, did he raise his head and take a glance at him with his ocean blue eyes from under his white brows.

'Good morning,' Alexander greeted him happily.

'Mornings are always good.'

The old man exhaled the last puffs of smoke and he stuck the long black pipe into his belt.

Alexander tried to argue with the old man, trying to prove that morning was nothing without night as light was nothing without shadows and darkness, but soon he was confused in his own thoughts. Alexander then asked the stranger, where his other house was, but didn't understand anything from the answer. The old man said that it was on the bottom of a pond. He didn't go into details, and Alexander thought that something was wrong. Alex had breakfast alone, dates, fruit and berries brought from the desert. He did not want to ask, but he guessed that meat was not allowed in the hut.

'Why aren't you eating anything?'

The old man laughed and revealed another secret. 'I'm not a human, Alex! I am also created in His image, but I have other virtues. I never eat or drink anything. I do not need it. My strength comes from nature and from the leaves I smoke. These leaves are not common tobacco. Few have seen the flower the leaves of which I smoke. The flower grows under the element of the universe that you are not aware of. It absorbs and receives power from the stars and the earth. This power remains in it, and when I smoke it, some of it passes to me. I have discovered recently that it is useful for humans and animals as well.'

He pointed to a small, thick, almond-shaped purple leaf. He said that many years ago it had helped him cure Momo, who had been fighting with a lynx. As a result, not only did his beloved cat survive, but also managed to live until now and be much stronger and bigger that ordinary cats. Moreover, he had prepared the potion with those leaves for Alexander, and he had recovered.

'Does it mean that I will live such a long life as Momo?' Alexander jumped up in fear, yet with joy.

The old man reassured him and said that only God gave every second of his life, and not the flower that was created by him as well.

'Take it as it comes. If you should live for a thousand years, you will live without that flower. It doesn't matter how many years you will be given. What matters is how you will fill these years. Nothing is impossible for the Creator of all and everything. Remember that!'

When they had finished talking and eating, Alexander asked him to reanimate the picture so that they could check the seedlings of the previous day. But the old man said that everything was fine there, and he wanted to show Alexander around the forest. He happily agreed, and they left. On the way, the old man was telling about the forest, about when and how it had appeared. Alexander was listening attentively and followed him. When they arrived at a meadow, the old man stopped and said that the whole area used to be like the meadow, only covered with grass and some bushes.

The old man warned Alexander not to be afraid and not to make sudden movements. At first, Alexander did not understand what he was talking about, but nodded. And the old man looked around as if smelling the air like a hunter. Then his eyes focussed at some point on the other side of the meadow, and he called. It was like a call with which people usually called each other when they were far away.

'Euuu, eeei...!'

Alexander found it so ridiculous that he couldn't help but smile. He lowered his head and was laughing under his breath. The old man felt that his call was heard. Alexander did not know yet that a pack of wolves, like happy dogs, was rushing towards them. With their tongues out the wolves were running through bushes to the beloved call trying to overtake each other. Like a bunch of flying arrows, they were swooshing ahead, every now and then disappearing in the tall grass and instantly reappearing to dive into the wild meadows again. Shortly thereafter, Alexander began to hear their voices. It took him some time to guess that it was a pack of wolves, but when he did, the smile froze on his face at once.

'This is the voice of wolves, isn't it?' he uttered in horror, not knowing what to do. 'What are you doing? Let's go before it's too late.'

'It's already too late,' the old man comforted him with a laugh.

He was laughing but trying to reassure the young man at the same time, saying that Alexander was safe next to him, and the wolves would not harm him.

'Don't be afraid, Alex, stand still and do not make any sudden movements. I didn't cure you to make you prey to the wolves. Calm down!'

Soon the first wolves reached the meadow. A giant grey wolf was running ahead of others. He was dashing like a flying arrow, staring at them. Soon the second, the third and the rest appeared. More than twenty wolves ran happily towards them, barking like dogs. Alexander was white as snow; not only was he speechless, he seemed breathless as well. He stopped thinking; his thoughts were gone, and he could not take his eyes off the pack.

When they approached the old man, the wolves seemed to have turned into dogs. They were licking his hands, rubbing up against his feet and greeting him happily. Alexander stood a few steps away and could not believe his own eyes. The wolves kept looking at him with cold eyes, came up to smell him, circled cautiously around him and went back to the old man. Full of envy, Alexander was watching the old man fearlessly and selflessly play with the wolves. It looked like a real fairy tale. Alexander wanted to go and play with them too, but he didn't dare. He felt that the wolves were looking at him differently. They didn't harm him and wouldn't harm him, only thanks to the old man. It was inexplicable and touching to Alexander's soul.

'Well, do you see wild animals in front of you, Alexander?'

The wolves didn't behave like wild animals at all. They were circling around the old man with great love, so Alexander began to doubt if love was innate also to animals.

'Come on, don't be afraid! Come, make friends with them…'

Alexander approached hesitantly, and the wolves surrounded him. They were sniffing him, pushing him with their muzzles, but did not harm him. A few minutes later, Alexander and the old man were sitting on the grass, while the pack was walking around them peacefully and cheerfully.

Alexander felt as if he was in a fairy tale. He was looking around and realizing that there was another world besides his own. It was not hidden and not too far to be beyond his reach. This world had always been by his side, but he did not notice it. It was so wonderful and so beautiful that deep inside Alexander wanted to live like the old man. And even if everyone thought he was crazy, it wouldn't bother him, a jot.

'They say, wolves are the most untameable animals. Maybe it's true, but they are not wild. People just don't see what they don't want to.'

'How could you?'

'So can you. But, first of all, you have to want it.'

'I do want it, but something is missing. Help me to see, as you can see, and to hear as you do.'

'I'll help you, Alex, but you've already been gifted, and you just need to realise it. When you do, you will begin to see and hear. There's no virtue that I can gift you with. You can be gifted with virtues only by Him.'

Then the old man got up and said that today they should see the forest. He said that the forest, unlike the desert, could not be seen at distance. Then he added, 'But for you to see it better, I'll show you the forest from above. Hold me tight!'

Saying that, he took Alexander under his left arm as lightly as a little sparrow. For the first time, Alexander felt his infinite power. Then, when he nodded in response to the old man's question, the old man bent his knees slightly and pushed himself off the ground with great force. In an instant, they took off. It took Alexander's breath away and his eyes filled with tears, and in a second, they reached the flight of the eagle. The old man could fly as easily as the fish could swim. He made no effort. It was enough for him to look at a point, and his inner strength immediately pushed him towards it. The wind blew in Alexander's face, and tears of joy welled up in his eyes.

'Do you see it's huge?' asked the old man, pointing at the forest stretching up into the mountains, which looked much more beautiful from above. Alexander didn't notice this at first. He was as thrilled as a child with a sense of flight. When they had left several miles behind, Alexander started listening again. He saw how beautiful the Earth was from above. Below the snow-capped peaks, the slopes were covered with red, yellow and brown forests. The base was covered with greenery. On the high slopes, belts of evergreen were scattered covering the bare mountains. They travelled a long way circling in the cold air. A pond, bluer than the sky, appeared in the distance. Alexander learned that the old man had created the pond by changing the course of the river. It took him a long time to direct the river into the gorge between the mountains and to form a lake there.

The old man told it in every detail and explained why he had done it. It all seemed incredible to Alexander, but he couldn't help but believe. He was floating under the old man's arm, and a cold wind was blowing in his face. This was not a dream.

'Do you mind if I call you "Painter"?' Alexander asked suddenly.

'Painter? But why, Painter?'

'Now I know what the Earth was like; it was shapeless and empty. You are a true master, and your canvas is the world. You are drawing on the surface of the earth. Your paintings are not dead; they breathe and move. You spread your paintings before God and His angels.'

The old man smiled. He really wanted the angels to look down and not to see the world naked and dull. He knew that there were no such colourful paintings on any of the countless other planets. Indeed, he was one of the few who painted on the surface of the Earth for the heaven.

He agreed, and from that moment on Alexander called him 'Painter. He told Alexander that the hut in the gorge was built long before the formation of the lake. It stood on pillars and looked like a dome. The entrance to the hut was from its floor, where the columns firmly held the floor and the base of the house. That was why, the water didn't get inside, and there were no windows either. But Painter didn't speak much. He made a circle and flew back to the forest. Alexander made him feel happy, and for some reason, he had no doubts about him any more. He was not worried about Alexander keeping his first promise and did not regret what he had done. Alexander had a kind heart and a free spirit. It was what really mattered, and Painter decided that he would give him more. But before that, Alexander himself had to strive for it. And for a reason known only to him, Painter told Alexander something that was very unexpected for him.

'I'm glad you understood everything. Tomorrow I will take you to the nearest settlement, so that you can return home.'

Those words seared into Alexander's heart like a red-hot iron. He didn't want to believe his ears. *Now, after all this, how can he expel me and send me back there…? Is he punishing me for something I did wrong?* Alexander thought, and the idea upset him even more.

'Why are you driving me away? Please, let me stay. I don't want to go.'

'You were born in the city, you are a human, and your life is there. You must go. Your loved ones are waiting for you. Have you forgotten about them?'

'You told me yourself that I want freedom, that I must open myself up and be like you.'

Alexander begged for some time, not to be driven away. These two days he had spent with Painter were more precious for him than the years before them.

'The only family I have are my parents who live in the US. You are my teacher. Teach me! I don't want to stay halfway.'

'You haven't opened yourself up yet, Alex! You can do it yourself. But for this you have to fulfil the second condition.'

'And what or who should I be afraid of?'

'They will try to stop you.' A desire to argue arose in Painter's eyes after his short reply.

Although Alexander was confused for a moment, he felt safe next to Painter. 'I will not be afraid as long as you stay with me,' Alexander said firmly.

'So, you have to purify yourself and stay alone. I will help you, but you need to open your soul and make a choice. Just remember that the choice is your gift, not your burden. This is a great virtue, as great as my virtues are. When you understand it, you will come closer to the truth. Now I must leave you alone until tomorrow. If you don't change your mind before then, I will take you where you can make a choice.'

Having said this, the old man opened one of the walls of the hut facing the mountains and was gone.

Alexander did not know what awaited him but was ready for anything. Maybe he would be in the desert, where he should stay alone, or somewhere else. It was not important. Alexander just wanted to get back to basics and start everything over. Not all that Painter said was clear or acceptable for him. He had discovered a new world that was too big and too deep to be understood. It was possible only to feel and to love it, believing that it was not a dream. He again remembered everything he had heard from Painter. The stories took

Alexander far, far away, where everything was very simple and incomprehensible at the same time. He hardly slept that night.

# The White Hut in the Desert

*The silver of the moon means that cold days are coming*, the young man sitting on the doorstep of the hut, thought suddenly. For a moment, he left Painter alone, and his mind was absorbed with the sounds coming from the forest. These were the sounds of a canvas created by Painter, the sounds of life. Alexander remembered the sounds of canvases created by people, the sounds of cities. These were not the sounds of life. The howl of the forest wolves could not even be compared with the noise of the lifeless cars that all the cities were full of. In the city, cars were always rumbling and honking, had to obey people and exactly follow their orders. The sounds of the city announced something terrible that people could not hear. All that created horrible pictures in Alexander's imagination.

The night is usually secretive, but there, on the threshold of the hut, it revealed one more secret to Alexander. When the images disappeared and Alexander could only hear, he once again was convinced that there was life in Painter's paintings. No matter how well people illuminated the cities they had created, they would never come to life, and no matter how dark the night was in a dense forest, life would always be felt there. Therefore, there is nothing relative, and Alexander tried in vain to convince Painter that even light was relative.

'Without darkness and shadows, light is still there, and it is good,' Alexander realised that night.

Painter told him that light did not cast a shadow, and the shadow consisted of the lightless bodies that stand, like a wall, in the path of light and block its passage, spreading part of its darkness on the path of light. But Alexander did not understand until he saw it with his eyes closed. He saw how beautiful the forest was during the day from a bird's eye, and how beautiful it was now, even when you couldn't see it.

The night lured and carried Alexander's thoughts far away, where there were no shadows and no doubts. Alexander did not realise how his eyes closed and if all he saw that night was a dream. Meanwhile, the night took him by the hand and led him to the seemingly unreal child's world, where there were no shadows.

When Alexander opened his eyes, he felt a heavy load on his shoulders, as if the world was pressing on him with all its might and threating to crush him. But Painter stood before him, and Alexander knew that he would never return, no matter how hard the trial was.

They reached the lake when it was past noon. On the way, Painter hardly uttered a word, and for some reason Alexander did not speak. He walked by his teacher's side, and this time he had no thoughts in his head. Having reached the pond, Painter stopped and looked at the blue mirror of the water. He was looking at the barely visible waves of the water, as if into someone's eyes, deep and determined. Alexander sat down on the shore. He didn't know why they had stopped or why they were waiting.

The old man could hear and see the whole lake. He heard the calm breathing of the pond and understood its every move. The pond was sleeping like a peaceful child. The wind was caressing its waves, and the earth was holding it in its arms so that no one would disturb the sleep of its beloved one. Painter did not wake it up either. He was waiting for the sun to send him a sign. He knew the language the universe spoke. During the day, he could see distant stars as if they were in his palm. Now he was speaking in that language and asking for something important for Alexander. He knew that before the sun went down and cast its rays on Alexander's face, he would see a shadow and speak to it. The moment was approaching rapidly and there was anxiety in Alexander's heart. Holy gates were opening over the horizon. Alexander could not see that. He did not see the brown gates on the other side of the lake, which were barely visible. Their shutters were higher than the treetops. They were opening with a terrible creak, and thick brown smoke was rising through the half-open shutters but not spreading around. It was merging with the thick gates, and if Alexander could see them, he would think that the gates themselves were made of thick smoke. But Painter saw. He was one of the guards against whose will nothing could get out of the gates. Chariots were heading towards him accompanied with the neigh of wild horses. These black horses were not reined in, but they obeyed the coachmen.

Painter was sternly watching the approaching chariots like a sharp-sighted hawk. The horse hooves did not touch the water. The horses were dashing toward the shore, circling in the air through the passage they had been given. It sometimes made the horses rise, lifting them up high above the lake's surface and sometimes lowering them to reach the water mirror. The dust also did not cross the invisible passage line. Painter scolded with his glance both the horses and their coachmen who were constantly trying to cross the line and spread into the forest. The pond was awakened by the unpleasant hoofbeats of the horses. Waves filled its blue surface as if trying to drive away the chariots, but Painter calmed the pond down.

Only one of the chariots approached Painter and stopped a few steps away from him. The coachman turned his horse and looked directly over his right shoulder at Painter, then his eyes turned to Alexander, who was sitting on the shore. There was complete silence. He looked at Alexander enquiringly. At the same time, there was hunter's caution in his eyes. Although Alexander did not see him, the coachman behaved like a hunting predator. The coachman, who was unusually tall and skinny, considered Alexander a human son for whom his dislike knew no bounds. Even his look made his eyes burn with hatred. And if Alexander was defenceless, he wouldn't hesitate to attack him, not even for a second. There was no conflict, because it was against Painter's will, and the aggressive coachman only smiled. His smile was familiar to Painter; he had seen it so many times before. It was like a bare moonlit slab that seemed to say, 'I will win again, and you know that.'

But Painter was motionless. He was as calm as his pond, and the coachman hated him for this calmness as well.

Painter was created for something else, and he did not fight against this army, although his deep blue eyes were burning with a passion for battle. He was ready to attack and to drown the countless chariots at the slightest sign. He was ready to push the shadow to the edge of darkness and to block its path forever. The coachman felt it too, and lines appeared on his face. The horses retreated with a roar, kicking up clouds of dust over the mirror of the lake. The gauntlet had been thrown down, and this was the beginning of a new story.

Soon the pond waved its mirror like the flag of freedom. The wild horses went running off its mirror and flew into the sky, but the sky shook them as well, and they went down the passage to the gates. When the gates closed, Painter's look changed. He looked towards the horizon again, then caressed the pond with his gaze.

Every now and then, Alexander gazed at him, waiting for his words.

Suddenly Painter spoke in a whisper.

'We are waiting for the sunset. When the sun reaches the horizon, the moment will come. The water will wash you, and by morning you will be purified. That's why it is worth waiting a little.'

Alexander wanted to ask but was lost for words. He understood that what Painter was saying was something important but secret for him. He decided to remain silent and to wait.

'When you are in trouble, remember that He is always with you. There you will be isolated from people and the world as much as possible, but He is always with you. Be like the one who prays even in his sleep, and this will help you.'

Painter gave Alexander some advice, and when the time came, he finally told him where he was going to take him. He felt the moment when the sun smiled at him. Painter asked the pond for help and to keep the doors open for Alexander. The pond smiled back at Painter and sent a light wave to his feet.

'You will stay in my hut under the lake. There is neither water nor air in it. But in this hut, I keep my flower I told you about. When you feel that your strength is leaving you, tear off one of its smallest leaves and eat it. That will keep you alive. One leaf will let you survive for a day. You might control the rest by yourself. So, come out, when the time comes; I will be here waiting for you.'

Alexander, didn't know what to say. He looked at Painter as if he wanted to hear from him that he would pull through. But there were no words of encouragement. Painter asked him if he was ready, and when Alexander nodded in dismay, Painter got him under his arm and took off. They quickly crossed the lake.

Alexander wasn't happy this time, though it might seem like an incredible pleasure in other circumstances. Now, he saw only cold water one or two steps below his feet, which had to become the first and the smallest hurdle in his test. They were flying fast, and for a moment Alexander had a wish to shout that he didn't want to go. His voice was stifled still in his throat, and when Painter moved several vertical hatches up in the centre of the lake, Alexander realised that they were to dive there. He managed to look at the decisive face of Painter for the last time, which lent him some determination, too. No sooner had Alexander taken a deep breath than he plunged his head deep into the cold water.

The sun was dimly illuminating the water. Alexander couldn't see anything, but felt that he was moving through the water at an unusual speed. Several seconds passed before Painter, with an abrupt movement, hurled Alexander through the opening in the floor of the hut just like stormy sea waves would wash a sinking ship ashore. Alexander found himself inside, but Painter was gone.

When Alexander came to his senses, he immediately stood up in a dimly lit hall, two steps away from the entrance. The opening was circular with a radius of about three feet. It was hard to breathe. Alexander had already noticed the flower, which was under one of the walls of the circular structure of the hall right in front of the entrance.

The flower seemed to have grown out of the floor. Its purple stem resembled the trunk of a dwarf tree. But as he got closer, Alexander noticed that the flower had actually taken root in the painted wall. Its countless golden leaves were softly lighting the hall like a candle. They were small but dense and smelled of a freshness that Alexander had never felt before. The flower was slightly taller than him. Its branches were covered with small purple leaves, through which wonderful flowers illuminated Alexander's face. They were so dense that the branches could be seen only in some places.

'So… that's what you look like,' he smiled.

The air felt stuffier, and Alexander tore off a little leaf gently, and put it into his mouth as if it was precious. He did not even want to chew it and decided just to swallow the sour leaf. It took several seconds before Alexander felt a huge amount of energy in his veins. The room became brighter, and even the breathing of the lake could be heard. Alexander got a clearer view of the hall. The walls here were also painted, but the whole room was covered with a single scene. It was a beautiful garden full of flowers and greenery. Two unusual trees were depicted facing each other. They rose above the greenery, spread out their branches in the semicircle of the room and touched each other only under the dome. They were separated by a white cloud, behind which Painter had hidden something. Alexander then noticed that there was an animal in the photo. Sheltered somewhere under the branches of one of the trees, a snake-like shadow was trying to reach for the fruit. Painter had intentionally overshadowed it, leaving only its vague outlines.

Alexander didn't know how long he had been examining the picture. He lost his sense of time and place. For some reason, the image had absorbed him and did not let go. Suddenly a thought flashed through his head, as swift and powerful as a spring thunderstorm in the mountains. Alexander blushed with fear, and his thoughts were confused.

*Isn't this the garden of Eden with the trees of life and wisdom? Sure, no doubt, it is the paradise. I feel it.*

Alexander had a feeling. In the depths of his soul, a warm star lit up. *Wasn't Adam created here?* Therefore, Alexander also felt at home here.

But the overshadowed figure frightened him. Alexander understood what was depicted there. Yes, before tempting Eve, the serpent was tempted to eat the forbidden fruit himself. But he ate the fruit of life. Now Alexander saw everything, he felt what was not written, and his heart was overwhelmed with great sadness. The room was revolving overhead, and Alexander fell to his knees under the starry sky.

The floor here was also all in stars. The universe was depicted as a peaceful sea with stars floating on it. Celestial bodies like countless boats were sailing in this endless sea, at times colliding with each other, but later were born anew.

Alexander seemed to see himself high in space, but at the same time in one of the countless boats on the earth. He did not even dare to think that Painter could open the walls here too, and taking him by the hand, make a step into the garden. He saw the miracle flower and realised that its roots were there, and the miraculous leaves received their strength from the paradise. Alexander was sailing in his boat for a long time. The universe was endless and full of secrets. He could neither win nor discover the infinite sea. He was just admiring it, sitting in a small boat. He felt like a passenger who could look out of the window. Painter had given him a ticket and put him in a boat, and now he was floating in space. Then he realised that Painter had only helped him to board the ship, whereas the ticket was given by someone else. Alexander was both happy and sad at the same time. He was glad to have met Painter, and learned from him. He made friends with the wolves and travelled over the forests, watching their beauty. He had learned secrets that no one knew about, and experienced immense happiness. Who could have thought and believed all this?'

*Will I be able to pay him back by appreciating all his kindness, or will new golden bulls be born and destroy my soul? Painter and everything else then will turn into a haze in my mind. A beautiful dream that will fade away and disappear as suddenly as it came.* Then Alexander burst into tears. He couldn't understand why he, nothing extraordinary, deserved it all. Did he really deserve to see and feel it?

*How great His love is for us, which we do not deserve!... And how generous He is to us, who are mean, to us who don't even believe in His existence...*

Thinking about it, Alexander forgot everything. He forgot Painter and the hall, in which he was, even himself. Only then did he remember all this and understand what Painter had in mind when he said that first he had to cut himself off from the world.

Alexander only occasionally came to his senses when his body told him to rip off another leaf. He didn't know how much time had passed. He didn't even think about it. While praying, he felt cut off from the ground. Some current slowly lifted him off the floor and took him up. But, whenever he got distracted and thought about it, he immediately fell down and hit the ground like a stone. Then he would close his eyes again and open his heart, forget all thoughts and allow his soul to dominate over his consciousness. And something lifted him up again. It felt like a dream.

And once in this dream, someone quickly came up and pushed him. Alexander nearly fell upside down. His thoughts mixed up in his head, and for a moment he was lost. Alexander knew for sure that he was not alone. He felt that the intruder was hitting him incessantly, as if trying to break in. Fear gripped him. It was not like a bad dream, from which you could immediately wake up feeling relieved. There, in that dream, it was a delirium, which could disturb your sleep, whereas in the awakened state, it could engulf you and not let you go.

Alexander pressed himself against the wall in cold sweat and held his little cross tightly in his hands. A whisper like a cold wind blew into Alexander's ear, 'It's just a fig leaf, and it won't cover your nakedness. Leave it, leave it! You're ridiculous, just look at yourself. You rely on this crazy old man. He can't even help himself. You are smart. Let it go, let it go! Freedom is yours, take it and go away! Well, yes, yes…'

One more second, and Alexander would lose himself, forever indulging in delusions. In this vast sea, he would be alone and without a boat.

'Remember that you are not alone, He is always with you…'

Suddenly he was struck by the stern look of Painter, and he remembered his words. Indeed, if there were an obstacle, then He would be with him as always. The fear began to recede. Alexander stood up and there was no more fear in his eyes. Then he remembered, 'Be like the one who prays even in his sleep…'

Alexander began to pray. No sooner had he finished than he woke up, out of breath. He did not know when he had fallen asleep, or if he was asleep or awake. So, Alexander was left alone with himself. His thoughts were intertwining with the universe and carried him into the depths of the endless sea. A light breeze was either lifting or lowering him, and it seemed there was no end. Alexander had already understood a lot but felt that something important was still missing.

He fought selflessly. His mind stopped trying to understand it. He doubted no more! He saw as Painter did, but only himself. He knew that in order to understand the world, he first needed to understand his own self. And now, he saw himself before and now. It was like the roads he had walked, feeling unsafe and lost. Now Alexander could see these roads from above and himself on them, just like he saw Painter's canvas during the flight. But he could not see the end of the road on which he was standing now. It was foggy, and Alexander could not see through it. The past was what it was. Sometimes beautiful, sometimes ridiculously funny. Previously, he was never left alone either on dark or light roads, but now he was at the most important crossroads. Alexander wanted to make the right choice but didn't know how to do it. The choice was difficult and full of surprises that were impossible to predict. Then he remembered other words by Painter. 'Remember that the choice is your gift, not your burden.' So, the path was not important, nor the companions. How you would walk through it was what really mattered. How and what would you choose at the next turn?

Sometimes Alexander walked around the hall, washed himself in the cold water of the lake and for hours enjoyed the beauty of the garden. Less and less often he was disturbed and distracted from his thoughts.

He was sitting with his back to the flower, his legs crossed, right at the round opening in the floor. Overhead were the trees painted by Painter. Alexander was struggling with his thoughts. They continued to convince him that he could get to the other side. But the river of truth was like a mountain river that blocked all attempts to get to the other side. Dozens of ideas and beliefs had already drowned in the whirlpools, and every now and then Alexander was pushed into and sank in the river of truth himself. He set foot in that river, over and over, trying to cross it. And the current beat him anew.

But one day, during a prayer, something invisible touched his head, as if stroking his hair and opening his soul. It seemed that his efforts were appreciated, and he was given the right to cross the river. This time he walked into the river without the fear of the current. He crossed it as easily as a flowing stream. But when he turned around and saw the bank behind him… the river was still mighty, and not everyone could cross it. Alexander quickly opened his eyes and just as quickly jumped into the well at the bottom. From now on, he was free.

He was a good swimmer and quickly moved towards the dim beams of the light. *It's good that it's afternoon now, and I can see the light*, thought Alexander, making his movements faster.

When he emerged from the water and saw the bright sun, he smiled at it and swam to the shore. It could be barely seen at distance, but Alexander was extremely happy. Against the background of the yellow forest, on the shore, he could see a white-haired man in a long blue robe. Alexander's tears mixed with the waves. He kept smiling until he reached and hugged the man.

Painter was smiling too. His deep blue eyes sparkled as he saw a new man emerging from the waves. Alexander thought that he had so much to tell Painter when they got to the hut… But when it happened, and he looked into the teacher's eyes, he realised that he could not say anything. They both knew all… Alexander knew that Painter saw immense gratitude in his eyes, and that it was pointless to express it. Painter could hear and read his soul, and Alexander preferred to keep it open to his teacher.

Alexander knew that he had to leave, and Painter knew it too. He bowed, then Painter read it in his eyes,

'Will we meet again…?'

The old man smiled. In his eyes, Alexander saw countless new days for himself. The roads were free and were waiting for the traveller. Alexander said goodbye. Momo, sitting on the fireplace, read something in Alexander's eyes for a long time. The king of the cats was not wrong this time either. His dark green eyes were pleased, and Alexander could not part with the white giant for a long time…

In the bustling city, Alexander walked like a wanderer. This was his birthplace, where every street was known to him. He looked at his hometown and at his friends who were rushing by. Alexander remembered the image he saw while under the pond, where he saw himself in the vast cosmic ocean, at the centre of navigation of countless stars. Now he saw everything differently, standing motionless on the surface of the Earth, surrounded by myriad crowds of people. From the stone sidewalks of the city grew entrapped trees, that reminded him of birds in cages, which he could not free. People covered the earth with stone and concrete and put shoes on their feet, as if to cut themselves off the earth completely. Alexander remembered Painter walking barefooted on the burning desert sand and gaining strength from the sand hot from the sun, as well as the story of Gilgamesh, cut off from the world by walls.

In the past, he, like many, was convinced that Vancouver was the most harmonious city in the world. It blended so well with nature with its gardens and parks that it seemed magical. But now everything was different. Alexander was walking along the sidewalks pressed between tall buildings and looking at the city from above. He saw it from the first day of its creation and fully watched its path. This path was different from the one he had chosen...

Due to his long absence, Alexander's employer decided to fire his irresponsible employee. Alexander was overjoyed to learn about it, having read one of the letters in his mailbox. He wouldn't have to go and talk to his employer for a long time. The second letter made Alexander even happier. His parents were doing well, and they were worried about him as always. Alexander read the letter with a smile but decided not to answer it. Anyway, his first duty was to visit them.

Alexander lived in a high-rise building. He could not stay long in his comfortable apartment. So, he climbed onto the roof, taking only a chair from the room with him. In his eyes there was the reflection of the streets with grey and cold faces. Giant skyscrapers had wrinkled the city's face. Cars and people were constantly making noise under them. Someone was running away from a car, and some people were being taken to hospitals. All this created a deafening noise, like a drumbeat in the hustle and bustle of a battle that drowned out the screams of those falling. The city drowned out the quiet begging voice of the world that only Alexander could hear.

Alexander was watching the commotion from a high rooftop and trying to find his place. He knew that there was no place for him down there, and that it was beyond his power to change what he could see below. Even Gilgamesh could not do it in the city he had built himself. Leave alone, Alexander... He stayed there for a long time, until the forgotten mobile reminded him of itself from the pocket of his jacket. *I have even forgotten about you*, he thought.

After the accident, all the gadgets of the civilised world had remained in the car, and Alexander had learned to live without them. But life in the city had different rules, and Alexander was reluctant to obey them. The call was from Bob, Alexander's best friend since childhood. They knew each other well, and Bob had been worrying about Alexander. He hadn't been able to reach him for several days.

'Alex, damn you, where are you?' Bob's voice sounded as cheerful as ever.

'In my room. What's up?'

'What's up? Come to our bar. I have something to talk about. I'm already here.'

Alexander hung up and jumped off the back of the chair he was sitting on. Then the elevator was taking him downstairs for a long time, and Alexander finally left the building. The red and green traffic lights took some time as well, sometimes stopping him and sometimes letting him move forward until Alexander got to the bar.

In a dimly lit hall, Bob's red hair seemed dark brown, but his always curious eyes remained the same.

Bob's character and his eyes were alike. He constantly came up with new ideas and shared them with Alexander, hurried and looked for horizons, known only to him, without leaving the city. Maybe that's why these ideas remained just ideas, Bob's ideas.

When they hugged each other and sat down at their favourite table in the basement, Bob enquired with his unique enthusiasm. 'Well, old buddy, speak up! Where on earth have you been?

To Bob's delight, it was a smoking section, and he was constantly fiddling with the smoking cigarette between his long fingers. Bob kept moving his hand as he spoke. As a rule, it moved in tune with his voice and the sequence of his ideas, as if it were his second language. Alexander briefly told him that he had had an accident but was not injured, so he had decided to stay in a beautiful location near the crash site.

Bob smiled, 'Buddy, are you really crazy? Everyone here was going to put out a search for you. If I did not lie that you had called me and that everything was fine with you, your vacation would not have lasted long. Yes, Al, especially your beloved boss. That idiot kept calling me non-stop. Have you spoken to him? What did you say?'

'Nothing. I'm free,' Alexander said in a very calm voice, bringing a heavy glass of beer to his mouth.

'What are you going to do now?

'Nothing! Anyway, I am out of the race.'

'Race? What race?'

'A horse race,' said Alexander slightly grimacing. Then, seeing the need for clarification in Bob's eyes, he added, 'We are like horses running around a racetrack, and our jockeys pay us for that. Good horses are taken care of, and those who get to the finish line last are thrown away.'

'Yes, man, you are right. Now the whole world is like that. So what? Have you finally decided to become a jockey?'

'No, it's even worse. It's no good being a horse, but the role of a horse torturer enriching oneself at their expense is even worse.'

Bob blew out a puff of smoke and put out his cigarette at the same time. He knit his brows tight over his eyes, narrow because of the smoke, and he asked Alexander in surprise, 'What are you talking about? It's as if you met a vegetarian girl who went deep into your mind and captured you. That is life.' As Bob said that, he threw up his hands, and there was deep conviction in his loud voice. 'Or do you want to open a religious group and preach all this? If so, don't rely on me. Instead, let's set up a political party or a movement. Yes, yes, you will attend drama classes and promise people a better future, and I will be your assistant.'

Bob, of course, was a cheerful communicator, but Alexander hadn't made his choice yet. And although he was talking and joking with Bob, his thoughts were somewhere else. People, drunk with the endless cigarette smoke, always talked about something "important" in the beginning, and then got carried away talking about nonsense; they were very depressive. Alexander realised that he was short of time. He knew that the city absorbed the powerful of this world and dragged them deep into the swamp until they sank. But Alexander didn't know where to run. The most likely places were the mountains, the islands of freedom or some village in the north.

His mind was abstracted from Bob's serious voice.

'Listen, if you really met the girl, send her to the hell as soon as possible before it's too late.'

'No, no, there is no girl. I'm just tired of all this. We work like slaves from morning to night for rubbish. We turn our time into money. We give a part of it to the state, and the other part becomes rubbish over time. The only difference between rich and poor slaves is the amount of their rubbish. The rich have more of it.'

'Come on, you really need to establish a party. I vote for Mr. Pellegrini.'

Bob jumped up, raised his right hand and shouted all over the place. Then he turned to the bartender, who was looking at him in surprise, like everyone else, and asked quite seriously. 'What about you, sir?'

'Me too,' he replied with a smile that revealed his white teeth.

'Yes, we all vote for Pellegrini…'

Bob would have continued the show if Alexander hadn't stopped him. This was typical of Bob, and Alexander was not surprised at all. Everyone in the place was smiling, except for the two men sitting opposite. Their displeased glances were visible even at the other end of the half-dark bar.

'Okay, Bob, stop it! Everyone is looking at us.'

'Let them look, do not deprive them of the small gifts of life.'

Bob's energy would suffice for the whole city. He understood Alexander but preferred to be a realist. And if he could choose, he would no doubt prefer to be, as he claimed, 'Among the lucky ones.' For Bob, giving up a comfortable life for the sake of going against the tide was complete nonsense. He had a kind heart, but, as Painter said, he hid it, like everyone else did. They were talking, and the lights in the forgotten city had been switched on for a long time. Bob tried to dissuade Alexander and explain that he was wrong. It was dawn by the time they said goodbye. Despite everything, he was always happy with Bob, and this time Alexander also managed to forget his thoughts for a while. Friends parted on condition that one day they would meet again. Alexander was looking at Bob nostalgically, although they hadn't parted yet. And for the first time, sadness could be noticed in the ever-cheerful look of his friend.

After visiting his parents, Alexander travelled for a while until he found his new hideout…

A lonely, untamed wind blew over the arid Mexican prairies. The wind was playing with the curls of a tall young man standing alone in front of a white hut built on a small hill. He glanced at the seedlings in the ditches that extended to the edge of the valley. The well pump broke the silence of the night, constantly pouring water into the ditches. The seedlings grew and so did the hut. Its low arched windows on all sides, no longer looked out onto the desert. And the curly-haired man standing in front of the hut was watching the children running in the shade of the garden. Only the wind was stroking his head.

The garden had changed the brown prairie, freeing up new lands. Alexander could no longer see the edge of his forest. When the wind blew from the north, he sent his warm greetings, hoping that the painting created by him would prolong the life of Painter and give him strength.

The End

# Epilogue

Jesus entered Jericho and was passing through. A man was there by the name of Zacchaeus; he was a chief tax collector and was wealthy. He wanted to see who Jesus was, but because he was short, he could not see over the crowd. So, he ran ahead and climbed a sycamore-fig tree to see him, since Jesus was coming that way. When Jesus reached the spot, he looked up and said to him, 'Zacchaeus, come down immediately. I must stay at your house today.'

So, he came down at once and welcomed him gladly.

All the people saw this and began to mutter, 'He has gone to be the guest of a sinner.'

But Zacchaeus stood up and said to the Lord, 'Look, Lord! Here and now, I give half of my possessions to the poor, and if I have cheated anybody out of anything, I will pay back four times the amount.'

Jesus said to him, 'Today salvation has come to this house, because this man, too, is a son of Abraham. For the Son of Man came to seek and to save the lost[1].'

---

[1] Bible. Luke 19:1-10

www.ingramcontent.com/pod-product-compliance
Lightning Source LLC
LaVergne TN
LVHW041539060526
838200LV00037B/1062